Barbie as The Island Princess

By Mary Man-Kong
Based on the original screenplay by Cliff Ruby & Elana Lesser

Special thanks to Vicki Jaeger, Monica Okazaki, Rob Hudnut, Shelley Dvi-Vardhana, Jesyca C. Durchin, Jennifer Twiner McCarron, Shea Wageman, Sharan Wood, Trevor Wyatt, Greg Richardson, Sean Newton, Kelsey Ayukawa, Luke DeWinter, Richard Dixon, Michael Douglas, Scott Eade, Derek Goodfellow, Shaun Martens, Chris McNish, Sarah Miyashita, Pam Prostarr, Craig Shiells, Sheila Turner, Lan Yao, and Walter P. Martishius

A Random House PICTUREBACK® Book
Random House 🏠 New York

Library of Congress Control Number: 2007902083   ISBN: 978-0-375-84218-4
www.randomhouse.com/kids   Printed in the United States of America   10 9 8 7 6 5 4 3 2 1

Long ago, a beautiful young girl named Ro was shipwrecked on a tropical island. With no other humans on the island, Ro was raised by some friendly animals: Sagi, the red panda; Azul, the handsome peacock; and Tika, the sweet young elephant. Together they became a happy family.

Ro loved Sagi, Tika, and Azul very
much, and each night she sang to them a lovely lullaby:
"It's magic when you are here beside me.
Close your eyes and let me hold you tight.
Everything that I could ever need is
Right here in my arms tonight."

One day, a handsome prince came to explore the island. He was amazed that the young woman could speak to animals!

"Where did you come from?" he asked.

"Sagi tells me I came from the sea a long time ago," answered the girl. "My name is Ro."

The prince was enchanted by Ro. "My name is Prince Antonio," he said. "Will you come back to the kingdom of Appolonia with me?"

Ro agreed—as long as she could bring her animal family along. During the journey, Ro and Antonio started to fall in love. And soon the prince dreamed of making Ro his princess.

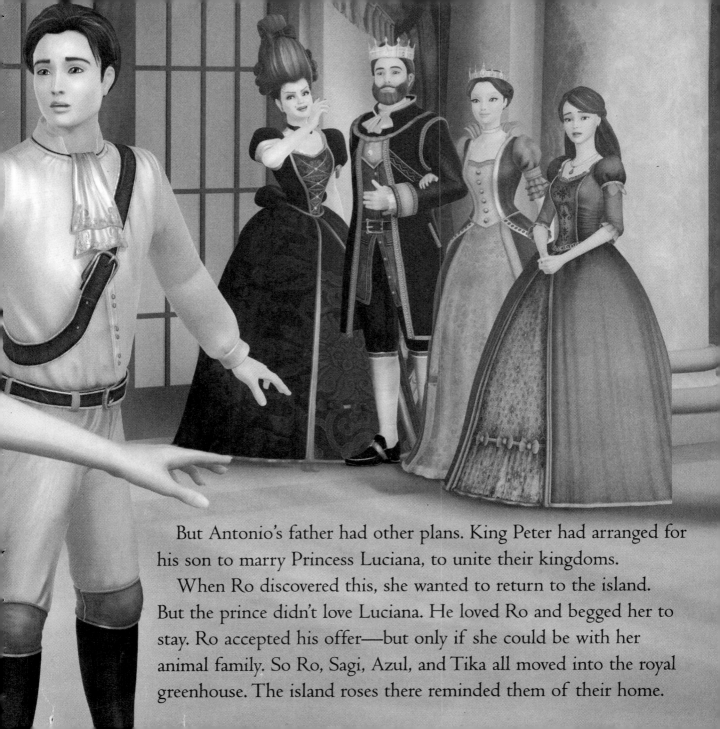

But Antonio's father had other plans. King Peter had arranged for his son to marry Princess Luciana, to unite their kingdoms.

When Ro discovered this, she wanted to return to the island. But the prince didn't love Luciana. He loved Ro and begged her to stay. Ro accepted his offer—but only if she could be with her animal family. So Ro, Sagi, Azul, and Tika all moved into the royal greenhouse. The island roses there reminded them of their home.

Queen Ariana desperately wanted her daughter, Luciana, to marry the prince—but for a different reason than King Peter. Long before, after failing to take over the kingdom, Queen Ariana and her family had been banished to live on a pig farm. Ever since, Ariana had vowed revenge. With her daughter married to the prince, Queen Ariana would finally overthrow King Peter and control his kingdom!

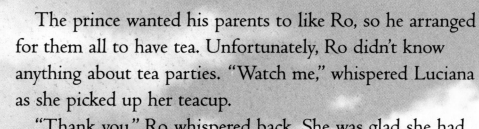

The prince wanted his parents to like Ro, so he arranged for them all to have tea. Unfortunately, Ro didn't know anything about tea parties. "Watch me," whispered Luciana as she picked up her teacup.

"Thank you," Ro whispered back. She was glad she had found a friend.

The next day, King Peter held an engagement ball for Prince Antonio and Princess Luciana—and everyone in the kingdom was invited. Ro had never been to a ball before. She was excited, but she didn't have anything to wear. Luckily, Queen Danielle's monkey, Tallulah, offered to help. She and Sagi, Tika, and Azul created a beautiful gown.

"You're going to have a great time at the ball," Tallulah said.

As soon as Ro entered the ballroom, the prince couldn't take his eyes off her. "May I have this dance?" he asked.

Queen Ariana was furious! She wanted to make sure that Princess Luciana married the prince. So Ariana commanded her pet rats to sprinkle a sleeping powder onto the food of all the animals in the kingdom. Then she would blame Ro and her animal friends for spreading the sleeping sickness.

When the animals mysteriously fell asleep, King
Peter believed that Ro and her animals were
responsible for the illness—and had them all thrown
into the dungeon!

Prince Antonio demanded that Ro be released,
but the king would agree only if Antonio married
Princess Luciana. Sadly, the prince accepted.

Ro and her animal friends were quickly put on a boat back to their island. Unfortunately, Azul had eaten some of the sleeping powder, too! Ro recognized that the powder was made from sunset herb. "We need the island roses from the greenhouse to save him," she said.

Suddenly, the friends were knocked overboard. As the waves crashed around them, Ro remembered being shipwrecked.

"Don't give up, Rosella!" her father had told her.

"My name is Rosella," she said in wonderment.

With newfound strength and hope, Ro called to the dolphins for help.

At the palace, the wedding of Prince Antonio and Princess Luciana was about to start.

Meanwhile, Ro arrived at the palace and sneaked into the greenhouse. Just as she finished making the antidote from island roses, Queen Ariana appeared.

"How dare you interrupt the wedding!" Ariana cried.

Just then, a tiny bird told Ro that Ariana had put sunset herb in the animals' food and on the wedding cake.

Realizing she was found out, Queen Ariana fled toward her carriage.

Ro quickly threw a pike at one of the carriage wheels, and the queen tumbled to the ground—and into a pigsty!

Back at the palace, Ro quickly gave the antidote to all the animals, and they slowly awoke.

King Peter approached Ro. "I'm sorry I misjudged you," he said.

"Will you marry me?" Prince Antonio asked Ro. With Princess Luciana's blessing, Ro agreed. "But please call me Rosella. That's my real name."

Just then, a wedding guest who had overheard came to them. "I had a daughter named Rosella," Queen Marissa said. "But she was lost at sea."

Ro started to softly sing her favorite lullaby:

*"It's magic when you are here beside me.
Close your eyes and let me hold you tight. . . ."*

*". . . Everything that I could ever need is
right here in my arms tonight,"* Queen Marissa finished.

"Mother!" Ro cried.

Soon the wedding of Prince Antonio and Princess Rosella
was held at the palace.

Prince Antonio married his island princess, and they lived
happily ever after——with all their family beside them!